Halle and Tiger
with their
Bucketfilling Family

By Peggy Johncox • Illustrations by Megan D. Wellman

Ferne Press

Halle and Tiger with their Bucketfilling Family
Copyright © 2011 by Peggy Johncox
Second Printing 2013
Illustrated by Megan D. Wellman
Illustrations created with colored pencils and watercolors
Layout and cover design by Kimberly Franzen and Raphael Giuffrida
Printed in the United States of America

In the 1960s, Dr. Donald O. Clifton (1924–2003) first created the "Dipper and Bucket" story that has now been passed along for decades. Dr. Clifton later went on to coauthor the #1 *New York Times* bestseller *How Full Is Your Bucket?* and was named the Father of Strengths Psychology.

Summary: When a new cat named Tiger comes to live with a dog named Halle, she must teach him how to live a bucket filler's life.
Library of Congress Cataloging-in-Publication Data
    Johncox, Peggy
    Halle and Tiger with their Bucketfilling Family/Peggy Johncox – First Edition
    ISBN-13: 978-1-933916-75-0
    1. Juvenile fiction. 2. Self-esteem. 3. Bucket filling.
    I. Johncox, Peggy II. Halle and Tiger with their Bucketfilling Family
    Library of Congress Control Number: 2010939738

FERNE PRESS

Ferne Press is an imprint of Nelson Publishing & Marketing
366 Welch Road, Northville, MI 48167
www.nelsonpublishingandmarketing.com
(248) 735-0418

This book is dedicated to all bucket fillers, all those who bring joy to life for others and themselves, and especially to all our grandchildren: Julian & Jaden, Elijah, River & Harmony, Jada & Josiah, and their parents, Erin and Jeremy, Andrew and Brooke, and Matthew and Hana.

There are so many wonderful people in my life who have supported, encouraged, and taught me by example that to list them would be difficult, so thank you one and all. My deep gratitude and special appreciation goes to my husband, Gary, my whole awesome bucketfilling  family, and our pets, Halle, Tiger, and Jasper. Thanks to Carol McCloud, friend and author; Megan Wellman, illustrator; Kris Yankee, editor; Marian Nelson, publisher; and most of all my Lord, who gave us the message, the animals, and the inspiration. All of these have made it possible to spread the message that enriches our lives.

ortion of the proceeds from this book is
ng donated to missionary work.

"Halle," Gram said, "I see you and Tiger have met. How nice of you to share your spot with our new friend. Tiger jumped into Poppy's truck last night. We found out he didn't have a home. I hope you'll welcome him into our bucketfilling family."

Each of us has an invisible bucket. When it is full, it's filled with good thoughts and feelings.

"Bucketfilling family? What's that?" Tiger asked. "Maybe you could tell me."

Halle said, "I'll try. A bucketfilling family is one where everyone cares about everyone else."

When your bucket is empty, you feel unhappy.

"You're in my spot right now, but if we share it, that's bucket filling," Halle explained.

Sharing with others fills their buckets.

A van pulled up to the house and honked.

"The grandkids are here!" Gram said as she and Halle ran out to greet them.

Being happy to see people fills their buckets.

"Hi Gram," Elijah and Jada said together.
"We brought Jasper with us."

Playing outdoors fills everyone's buckets, even dogs'.

Elijah threw the ball for the dogs and said, "Jasper and Halle, can you fetch this?"

"I'm so happy when you come over and play with me," Halle told Jasper as they chased after the ball.

When you fill someone's bucket, your own bucket fills up too.

"We have a new cat named Tiger," Halle said. "Please don't chase him. He doesn't know you, and you might frighten him and dip into his bucket."

"Okay, I'll give him time to feel safe," Jasper said.

Dipping into someone's bucket is when you make that person feel bad.

As the children played, they petted and kissed the dogs.
Jada said, "Good dog. I love you, Jasper."

Love and kindness always fill buckets.

"Children, dogs, let's all go down to the pond now," Gram called. The children climbed onto a big inner tube. The wind began to blow them out too deep into the pond.

Unnecessary danger dips into buckets.

Halle barked a warning from shore. Jasper quickly jumped into the water and began swimming toward them.

Working together as a team fills buckets.

Gram called out, "Stay calm. Elijah, throw Jasper the rope. He can help you."

Jasper pulled them back to shore.

Following directions fills buckets.

Gram said, "Please be careful not to drift out so far. It's not safe."

Listening fills buckets.

"We're sorry, Gram. We didn't mean to scare you," said Elijah. "We forgot to watch, but the dogs rescued us!"

Apologizing to others fills buckets.

"Good dogs!" Gram said. "I'm so happy when we help each other and keep each other safe. Children, you are forgiven, but please be safe. Dogs, thank you for working so well together."

Giving thanks fills buckets.

Returning home, Tiger said to the dogs, "I saw what happened. You two are brave and smart."

"Thank you," the dogs said together.

Just then, Poppy came home from work, and Halle ran to greet him.

Giving compliments fills buckets.

Tiger jumped onto the stool and walked across the kitchen counter.

Gram was surprised and took him off. "No! No, Tiger! Cats can't go on here. Stay down. In this house, animals stay off of the counters and tables."

Disobeying rules dips into buckets.

As he hung his head, Tiger said to Halle, "I think I just hurt Gram's feelings. Do you think I dipped into her bucket?"

Halle nodded. "Yes. You'll need to apologize."

When we make mistakes, we sometimes dip into other people's buckets.

Tiger rubbed up against Gram's leg and purred.

"I forgive you, Tiger," Gram said.

Forgiving others for their mistakes fills everyone's buckets.

In the living room, Tiger found a red bandana. He took it into the corner and used it as a pillow. Tiger fell asleep quickly.

Rest and naps fill buckets.

"You stole my red bandana!" Jasper said.

Tiger opened one eye and said, "No, I didn't.
This was on the ground. It's mine."

Accusing people of wrongdoing
dips into their buckets.

"It must've fallen off. See the dogs on it? It's not for cats."

Tiger examined the bandana and then said, "You're right. Sorry about that."

Admitting when you're wrong or mistaken fills buckets.

"It was an honest mistake," Jasper said.

"I smell something good," Halle said. "Let's go see what it is."

Forgiving quickly fills buckets.

"Be careful," Halle warned. "When Poppy's at the grill, it's not good to be under his feet."

Thinking about the needs of others fills buckets.

"Wow, I have a lot to learn, but I can start by watching and listening," Tiger said.

"I'll stay here too," Halle replied.

You fill your own bucket when you learn something new.

"Hello, my friends," Poppy said. "Look at you sitting so nicely while I cook. Would you like a treat?"

Tiger purred loudly.

Treats and gifts fill everyone's buckets.

"What's that sound you're making?" Halle asked.

"It's purring—the sound of pure joy that cats make when our buckets are full!" Tiger said.

Being kind fills everyone's buckets.

"I like being in a bucketfilling family. Everyone is kind and helpful to each other," Tiger said. "Thank you for letting me stay."

"We're glad you're here," Halle said.

Your family fills your bucket, and you need to fill theirs, too.

Peggy Johncox has taught grades K–8 for thirty-three years. She has taught in several districts in Michigan, as well as in Title I classrooms and on Indian reservations in Arizona and New Mexico. In 2001, Peggy was the Teacher of the Year for Fowlerville Community Schools in Michigan. Peggy now delights in presenting the bucketfilling philosophy as explained in Carol McCloud's three books, *Have You Filled a Bucket Today?*, *Fill a Bucket*, and *Growing Up with a Bucket Full of Happiness*. "As we spoke with children, I observed how much our pets fill our buckets. Halle, our miniature pinscher, is a perfect, fun example to promote these desired concepts." Peggy lives in the woods of southeast Michigan with her husband, Gary, and their dog, Halle, cat, Tiger, and parakeet, Sassy. Peggy and Gary have three married children and seven grandchildren.

For more information about Peggy, please visit her website at www.peggyjohncoxbooks.com.

Megan D. Wellman grew up in Redford, Michigan, and currently resides with her husband, two Great Danes, and a cat in Canton, Michigan. She holds a bachelor's degree in fine arts from Eastern Michigan University with a minor in children's theater. *Halle and Tiger with their Bucketfilling Family* is Megan's tenth book. Her books include *Liam's Luck and Finnegan's Fortune*, *King of Dilly Dally*, *This Babe So Small*, *Lonely Teddy*, *Grandma's Ready*, *...and that is why we teach*, *Being Bella*, *Read to Me, Daddy!*, and *Does This Make Me Beautiful?*, which are all available from Ferne Press.